Big Brother Piggley

adapted by Jodi Huelin
images by Entara Ltd.

Ready-to-Read

Simon Spotlight
New York   London   Toronto   Sydney

Based on the TV series *Jakers! The Adventures of Piggley Winks* created by Entara Ltd.

SIMON SPOTLIGHT
An imprint of Simon & Schuster Children's Publishing Division
1230 Avenue of the Americas, New York, New York 10020

Manufactured in the United States of America
First Edition
2 4 6 8 10 9 7 5 3 1
Library of Congress Cataloging-in-Publication Data
Huelin, Jodi.
Big brother Piggley / adapted by Jodi Huelin ; images by Entara Ltd. — 1st ed.
p. cm. — (Ready-to-read)
"Based on the TV series Jakers! The Adventures of Piggley Winks created by Entara, Ltd. as seen on PBS Kids."
ISBN-13: 978-1-4169-2819-5
ISBN-10: 1-4169-2819-7
I. Entara Ltd. II. Jakers, the adventures of Piggley Winks. III. Title.
PZ7.H8696Big 2007
2006020319

It was a rainy day.

The sky was dark.

Fat rain drops

fell from thick .

CLOUDS

 was bored.

PIGGLEY

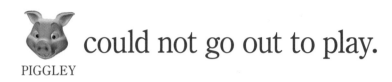 could not go out to play.

PIGGLEY

He could not meet up with

his friends and .

FERNY   DANNAN

He had to stay inside.

He read a .
BOOK

He made faces in a 🪞 .
MIRROR

He made a shadow puppet.

"The wind is strong," said .

MR. WINKS

"The 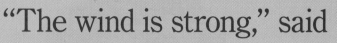 fell down.

FENCE

We have to fix it,

or the 🐑🐑🐑🐑 will get out."

SHEEP

"I will help you!" said .
PIGGLEY

"I do not mind the 🌧️ or 🟤."
RAIN   MUD

But  had other ideas.

MRS. WINKS

"I need you to stay in the

HOUSE

and look after ," she said.

MOLLY

"I will be the head

of the house!" said .

PIGGLEY

"The king of the castle!"

"We will have fun!" told .

PIGGLEY   MOLLY

They ran around the

HOUSE

as airplanes.

They jumped over

a pretend alligator.

They played a game of  .

CHECKERS

But  did not like

the pretend alligator.

She did not like to lose at .

CHECKERS

She ran outside to find .

MRS. WINKS

 **MRS. WINKS** was not happy.

She told **PIGGLEY** that he should not

beat his sister at **CHECKERS** .

That meant that he was not

playing **with**  .

MOLLY

"Being a big brother

is a big job," said.
MRS. WINKS

" looks up to you."
MOLLY

"I know," said  .
PIGGLEY

"I will be more careful

of her feelings."

 asked to read her a .

MOLLY   PIGGLEY   BOOK

It was a about a princess.

BOOK

But did not want to read

PIGGLEY

a about a princess.

BOOK

So he read her a  BOOK

about cowboys instead.

At lunchtime

 made a

PIGGLEY   MOLLY   SANDWICH

with  , and .

JAM   CHEESE   TOMATO

"You do not do it right!"  cried.

MOLLY

 understood what

PIGGLEY

his mom had tried to tell him.

 was little.

MOLLY

She did not like

the same things as .

PIGGLEY

So  tried to make

the day fun for .

He taught her to make

shadow puppets.

He taught her to play .

He read her favorite .

"I am proud of you, ,"

said .

"Being a big brother

is a big job," said .

"And I love it!"